This item was added to the
ME Library collection as a
benefit of the '07-'08
Scholastic Book Fair

P9-BYC-497

182.1
Coh

MUSKEGO ELEM. LIBRARY
S75W17476 Janesville Rd.
Muskego, WI 53150

★ YOU'RE A GRAND OLD FLAG ★

NORMAN ROCKWELL

You're a Grand Old Flag

LYRICS BY GEORGE M. COHAN

MUSKEGO ELEM. LIBRARY
S75W17476 Janesville Rd.
Muskego, WI 53150

ATHENEUM BOOKS FOR YOUNG READERS
NEW YORK   LONDON   TORONTO   SYDNEY

My grandfather, Norman Rockwell, was born in New York City in 1894 and died in Stockbridge, Massachusetts, in 1978 at the age of eighty-four. He witnessed the growth of the United States, watching it become the most powerful, dominant country in the world. Norman Rockwell's response to his country's growth and newfound power was to focus his art on the everyday aspects of life in America through depictions of the lives of ordinary Americans.

In 1913, my grandfather became the art editor of *Boys' Life* magazine, beginning a career in which he went on to produce more than four thousand works for magazine covers, book illustrations, and advertisements. His career flourished during an age when magazines were the mass media of the time, and most of their covers, interior illustrations, and advertisements were done by illustrators. Norman Rockwell's best-known works were done for the cover of the *Saturday Evening Post*. He completed three hundred and twenty-one covers from 1916 to 1963.

The present collection accompanies the song "You're a Grand Old Flag" and illustrates themes representing the spirit of the American flag. The book contains familial images—from the family in *Carrying On* to the humor of children eating corn or running from the swimming hole; from images of a larger American family in *Salute the Flag* and the sadness of those left behind in *Till the Boys Come Home* to depictions of the American adventurous spirit in *Man on the Moon*. The images in this book also show historical turning points in our nation's history, as with *Abraham Lincoln Delivers Gettysburg Address*, and quiet patriotism, as shown in the painting of a grandmother in the privacy of her home in *Mending the Flag*. These themes of Americana were dear to Norman Rockwell, and I believe he would be pleased with this collection and its pairing with "You're a Grand Old Flag."

—John Rockwell

You're a grand old flag,

You're a high flying flag

And forever in peace

may you wave.

You're the emblem of

The land I love.

The home of the **free**

and the **brave.**

Ev'ry heart beats true 'neath the

Red,

White,

and Blue,

Where there's never a

boast or **brag**.

Should

auld acquaintance

be forgot,

Keep your eye on the

grand old flag.

You're a **grand old** flag,

You're a **high flying** flag

And forever in **peace** may you wave.

norman rockwell

You're the emblem of

The land I love.

The home of the **free**

and the

brave.

Ev'ry heart beats true 'neath the

Red, White,
and Blue,

Where there's never a **boast**

or **brag**.

Should **auld acquaintance**

be forgot,

Keep your eye

on the **grand old flag.**

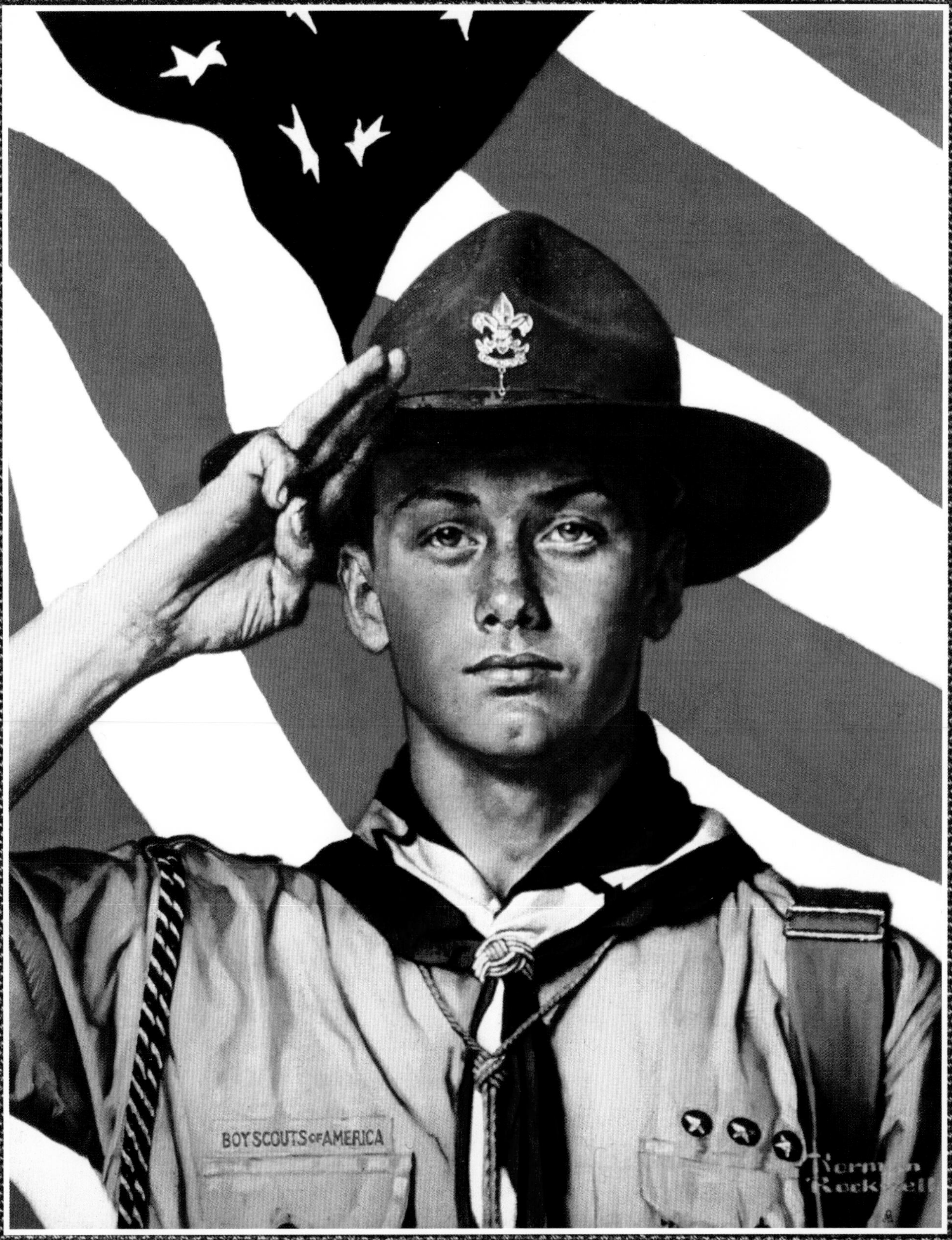
BOY SCOUTS OF AMERICA
Norman Rockwell

ILLUSTRATIONS CREDITS

p. 1
Carrying On,
Life cover, July 1, 1920
(NRM).

p. 2
Who's Having More Fun,
Green Giant advertisement,
1939
(NRFA).

p. 7
Oh Boy,
Literary Digest cover,
February 8, 1919
(NRFA).

p. 9
Till the Boys Come Home,
Life cover, August 15, 1918
(NRM).

p. 11
No Swimming,
Saturday Evening Post cover,
June 4, 1921
(NRFA).

p. 13
Salute the Flag,
Top Value Stamps, 1971
(NRFA).

p. 15
Boy with String,
Kellogg Co. advertisement, 1954
(Collection of Norman Rockwell
Museum, Stockbridge,
Massachusetts).

p. 17
Are We Downhearted,
Life cover,
November 28, 1918
(NRM).

p. 19
Man on the Moon,
Look cover, January 10, 1967
(NRFA).

p. 21
Mending the Flag,
Literary Digest cover,
May 27, 1922
(Photo courtesy of Norman
Rockwell Museum,
Stockbridge, Massachusetts).

p. 23
Boy and Dog,
Hercules Power Co. calendar, 1941
(NRFA).

p. 25
On Top of the World,
Ladies Home Journal cover,
April 1928
(NRM).

p. 27
Abraham Lincoln Delivers Gettysburg Address,
McCall's cover, July 1942
(NRFA).

p. 29
We, Too, Have a Job to Do,
Boy Scouts of America
calendar, 1944
(Photo courtesy of Norman
Rockwell Museum,
Stockbridge, Massachusetts).

All images reproduced with permission
from the Norman Rockwell Museum (NRM)
and the Norman Rockwell Family Agency (NRFA).

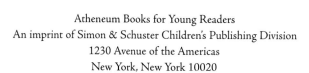

Atheneum Books for Young Readers
An imprint of Simon & Schuster Children's Publishing Division
1230 Avenue of the Americas
New York, New York 10020
Compilation of artwork copyright © 2008 by Norman Rockwell Family Agency
All rights reserved, including the right of reproduction in whole or in part in any form.
Book design by Krista Vossen
The text for this book is set in Adobe Jenson.
The illustrations for this book are rendered in oil on canvas.
Manufactured in the United States of America
First Edition
2 4 6 8 10 9 7 5 3
Library of Congress Cataloging-in-Publication Data
Cohan, George M.
You're a grand old flag / George M. Cohan ; [illustrations by] Norman Rockwell. — 1st ed.
p.   cm.
Summary: Norman Rockwell images accompany this patriotic song written for a Broadway musical by George M. Cohan.
ISBN-13: 978-1-4169-1770-0
ISBN-10: 1-4169-1770-5
1. Children's songs, English—United States—Texts. [1. Flags—United States—Songs and music. 2. Songs. 3. Patriotic music.]
I. Rockwell, Norman, 1894–1978, ill. II. Title. III. Title: You are a grand old flag.
PZ8.3.C655You 2008
782.42—dc22
[E]   2007025381